Blunderbuss Wanderlust

Bieng an Account of the Temporal Travels of Colonel Victor Von Vector

And the Eras of His Ways

By

David Shapiro and **Christopher Herndon**

First hardcover cover edition April 2016

Art direction and Cover by Christopher Herndon
Edited by Thea Kuticka

Library of Congress Cataloging-in-Publication Data

First hardcover edition ISBN: 978-1-940052-13-7.

First paper edition ISBN 978-0-98444-220-1.

Special Thanks to Daria Tessler & Thalyn Nikolau

CRAIGMORE CREATIONS

Portland, OR
www.craigmorecreations.com

Printed in Canada

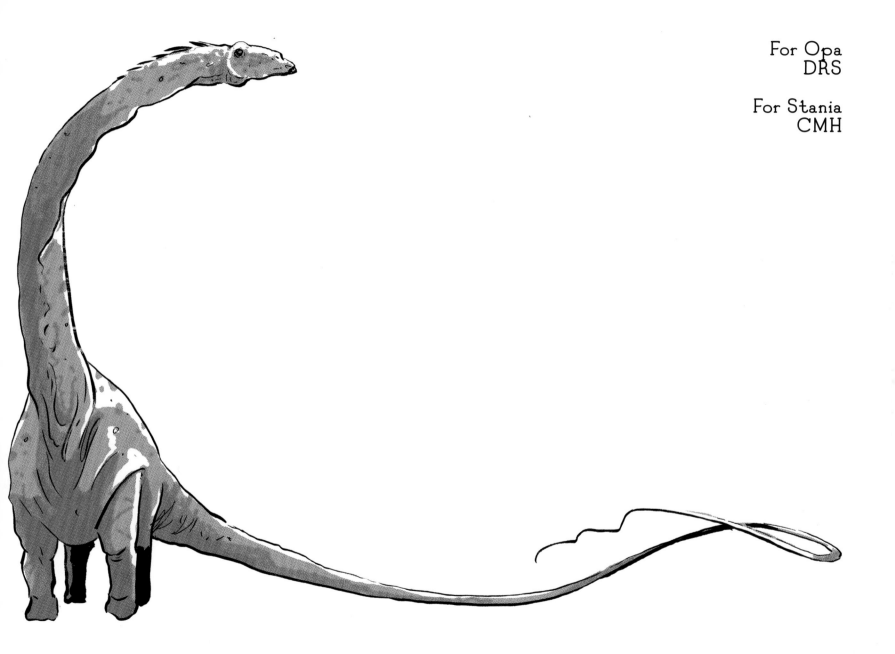

For Opa
DRS

For Stania
CMH

Victor am I and I traveled through time,
Due to my recoiling blunderbuss gun
Gifted to me from an old friend of mine.
This friend had a strange sense of what is fun.

From my study, on a blooming spring day,
I shot for the trees, no target to aim.
The recoil sent me well out of my way,
Six hundred million years ago I claim.

How do I know, I will tell unto thee,
Tales of the creatures I saw with my eyes.
When first I fell in the Cambrian Sea,
I could not breathe and I thought I would die.

I took a moment, then look'd all around,
In a place where Trilobites did abound.

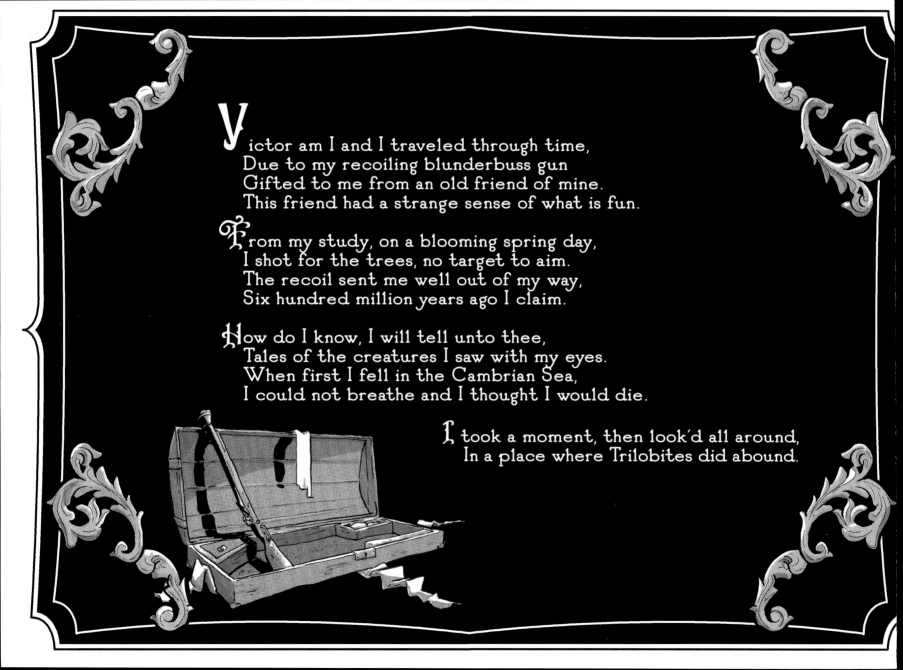

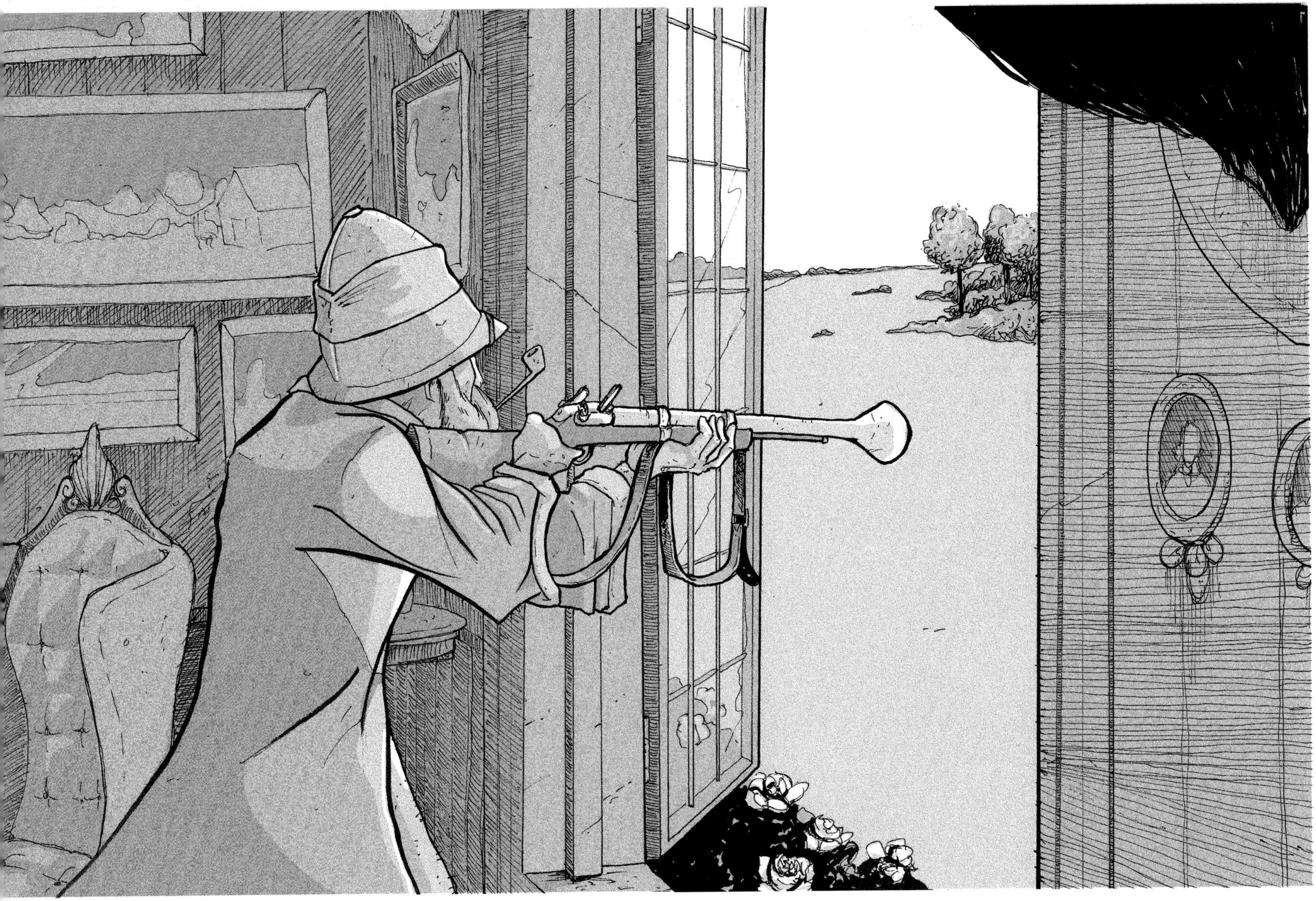

With little oxygen to respire,
My face began to turn a shade of blue.
I had to act fast or I would expire.
I fired my gun "twenty three skidoo."

Before the portal opened up for me,
I took in all the sights of early life.
An explosion of forms swam in the sea,
Diversity of species there was rife.

It would have been nice to gander around,
But nicer still would be a gasp of breath.
The pulse inside my head began to pound
Like Morse code with the message of my death.

So I took aim and shot my blunderbuss.
And understood, on this trip—be cautious.

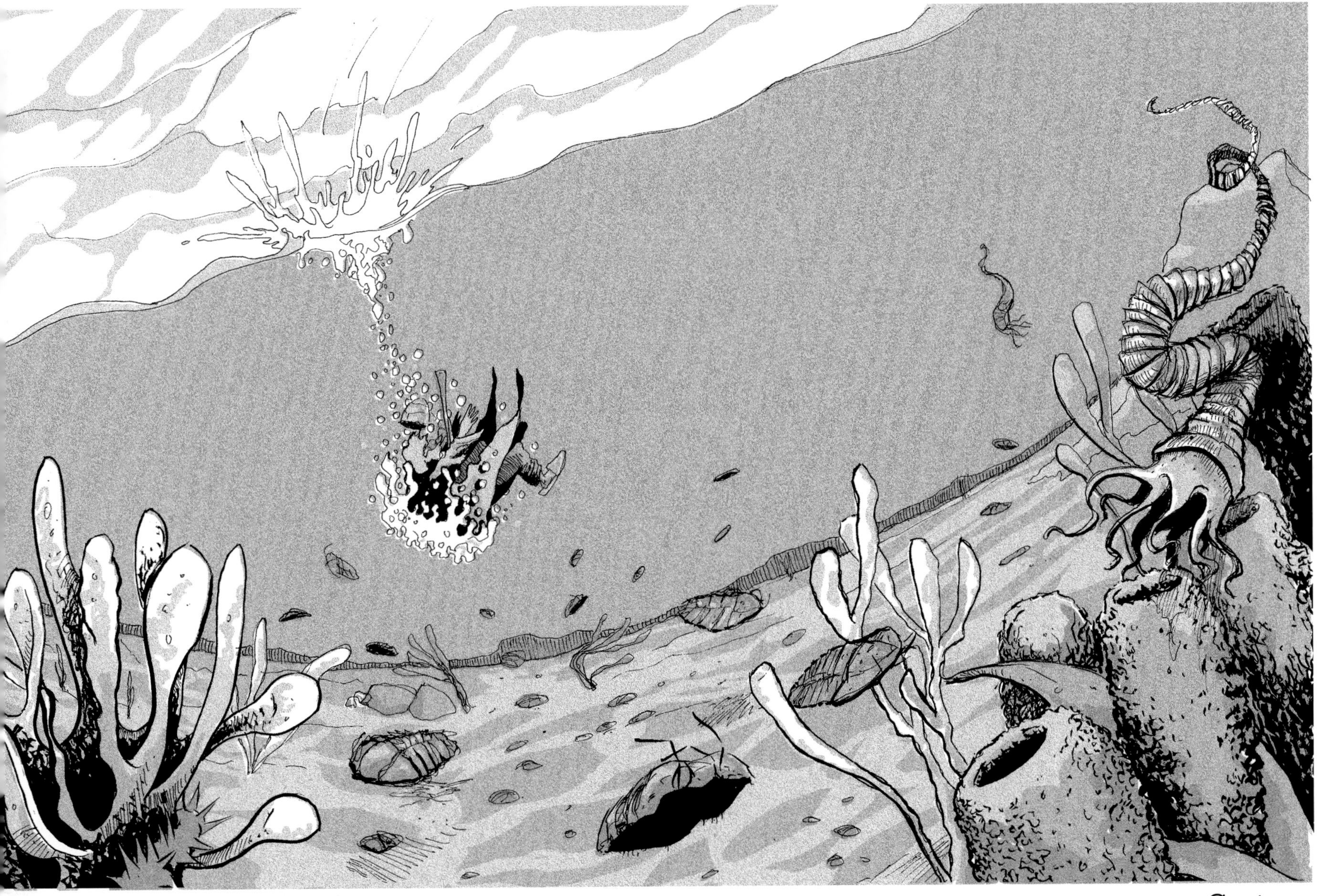

Cambrian
570 M.Y.A.

The Ordovician was my next stop.
I could tell time by the Orthoceras—
It was fourteen feet from bottom to top.
I gave it wide berth and stuff'd my cares.

Being a Colonel, my will is of steel,
Despite the fact I was about to drown,
I was not to be anything's next meal,
And lack of breathing could not keep me down.

I plodded through the developing sea,
Past Graptolite, Crinoid, Cephalopod too.
I'm afraid my stay had to end brusquely.
Steadfast in my resolve I pushed on through.

True to its form the blunderbuss sent me
Swimming again in an evolving sea.

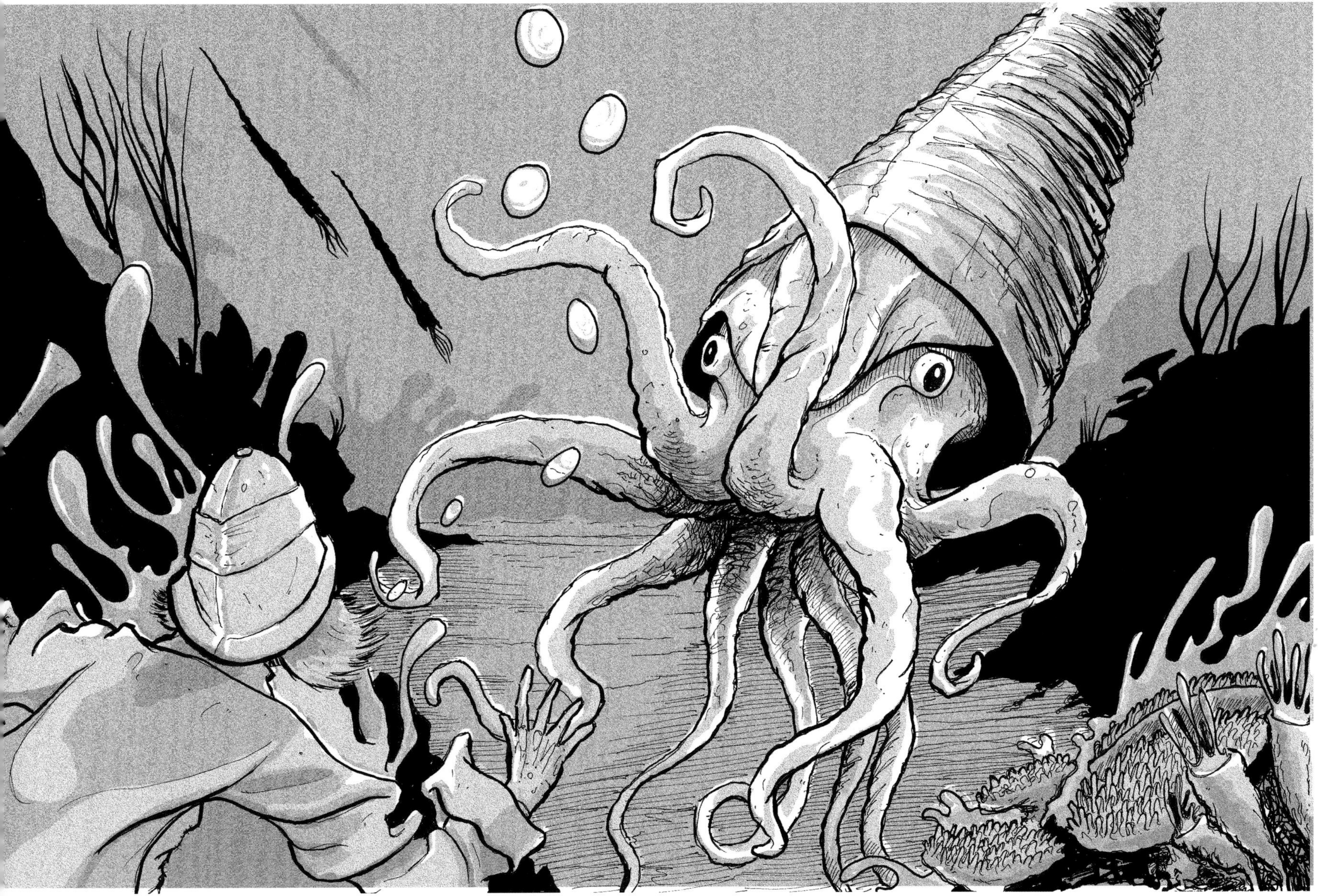

Ordovician
500 M.Y.A.

To the Silurian I did arrive,
Still in the ocean I `gain found myself.
A tale of this sort I could not contrive,
Of vibrant life o'er the continent shelf.

I swam in the shallow marine environs
With the early fish and Eurypterid.
My breath held tight as a cloister of nuns.
I would have traded my lot for two quid.

I had become weary of the ocean,
   Unsure of how much water I could bear.
   I reckoned I must discharge and move on,
      For I was in great need of some fresh air.

         The blunderbuss recoiled, time slipped away.
            Through the portal I went, to a new day.

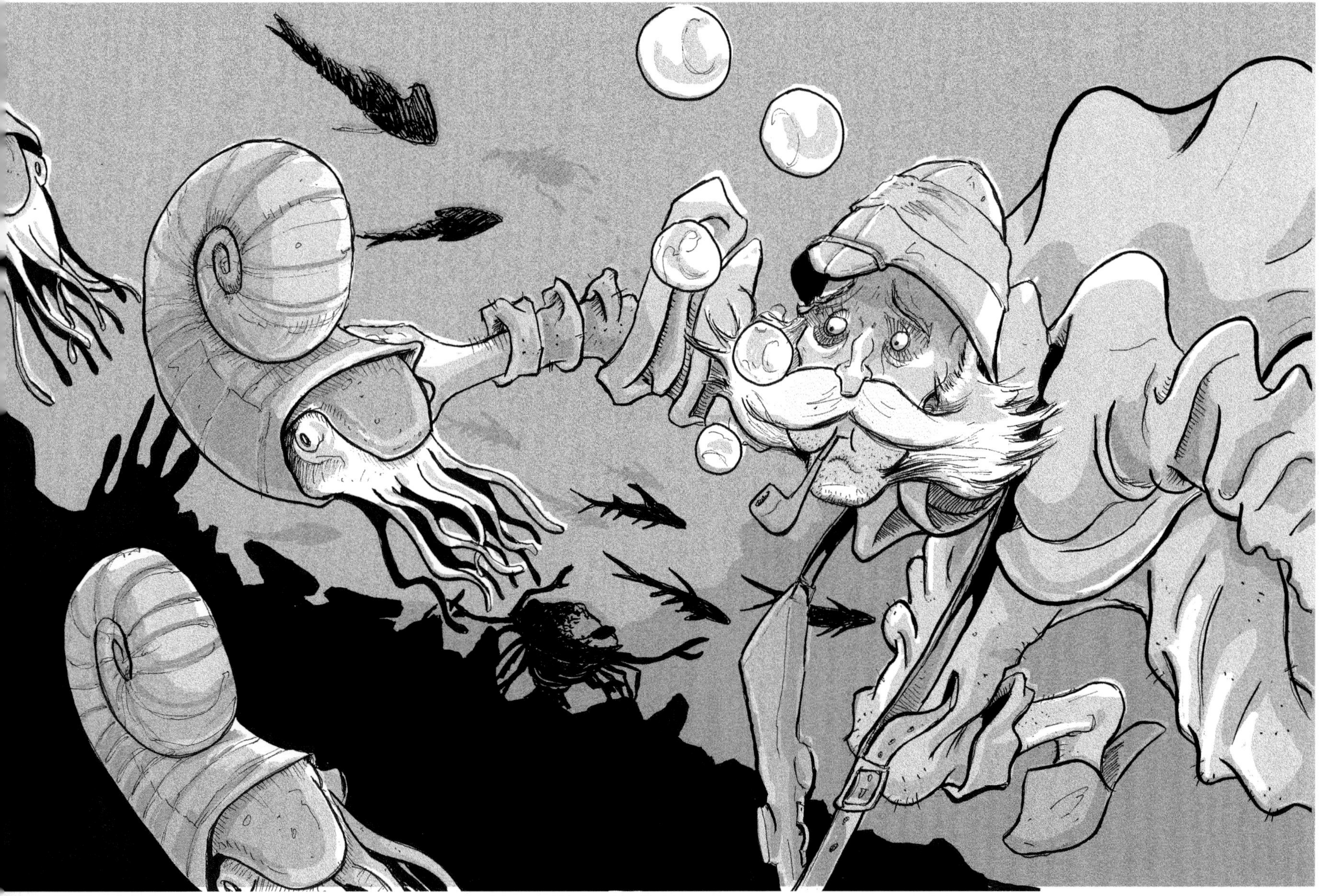

Silurian
480 M.Y.A.

In Devonian times I found myself next
Being chased by a large Dunkleosteus.
    To clarify my feelings in context,
    I was 'fraid to be eaten the mostus.

I swam like mad from the bony head beast,
    Making a straight line to the nearest shore.
    Not wanting to be a part of the feast,
    I swam much faster than ever before.

I left Leviathan out in the deep,
    And when I felt the sand with my own hand,
    I was so happy I wanted to weep.
    For I had arrived on the land, sweet land!

            Moreover than that I could finally breathe—
                You have no idea my sense of relief.

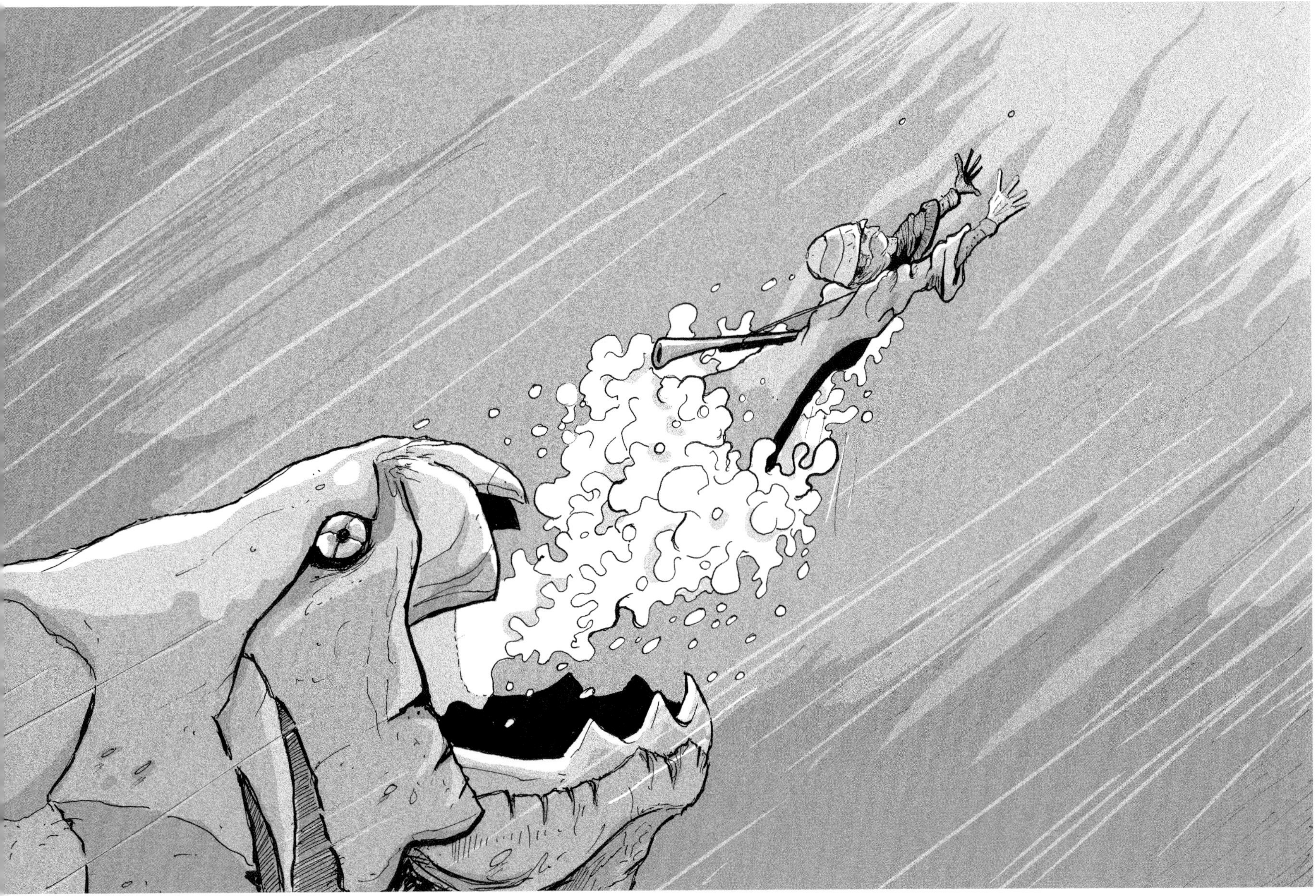

Devonian
395 M.Y.A.

On the beach at last I found my respite,
Before my eyes were able to adjust.
Lo, my breathing was still a labored fit.
There at my side was the strangest of busts,

Still half in the water as I was too.
T'was the great ancestor Tiktaalik,
Who was perhaps the first to bid adieu
To fins in favor of what became feet.

At this early stage of development
These "feet" were not used for walking at all,
But all the same and nonetheless nascent
In the quest for land, this fella had gall.

    The time had come to shoot the blunderbuss.
     I left Devonian times with no fuss.

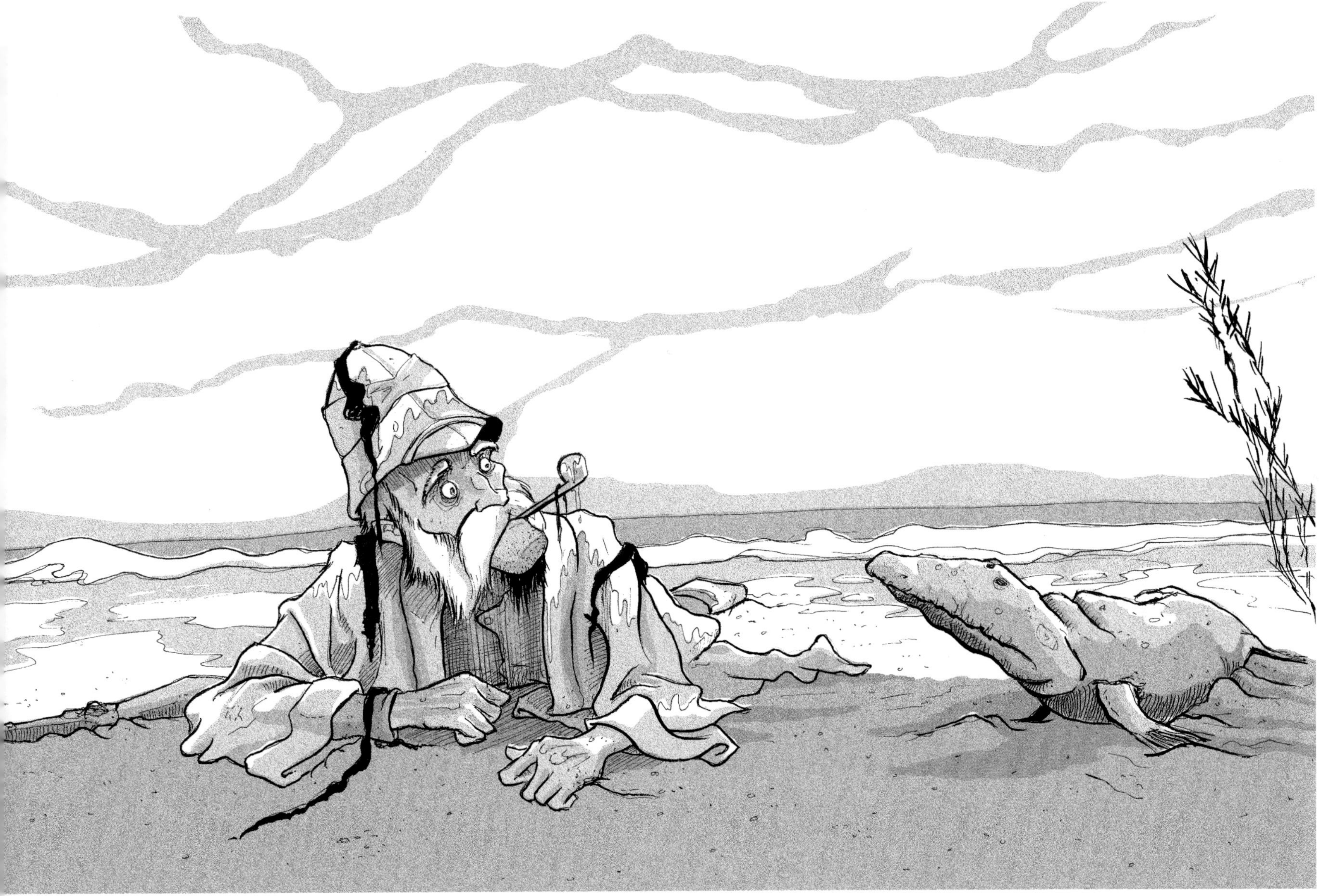

Devonian
395 M.Y.A.

The Carboniferous was my next rest.
The air was living rich with oxygen,
With verdant vegetation it was blest,
A great coal-producing ecosystem,

On account of all the fecundity.
Creatures now small were quite large at the time,
Like the dragonfly big as my body.
Oh, the strange sounds and wonders of this clime!

I trudged and I tramped till the day was long,
Looking with awe at this fantastic swamp.
The great ease of breathing drove me to song
That I sang to myself throughout the romp.

Colonel Victor Von Vector travels time,
Careful is he not to lose his good mind.

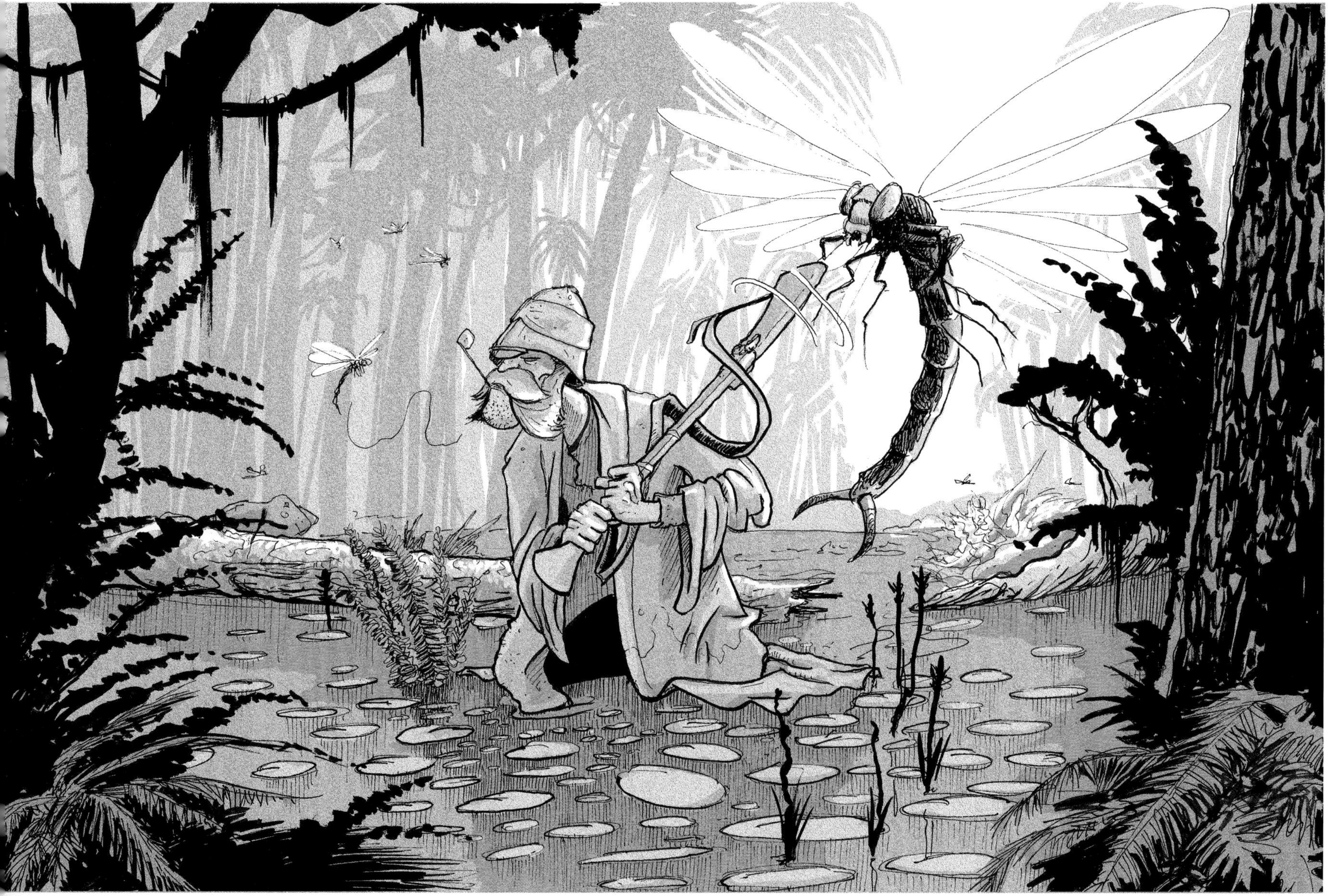

Carboniferous
345 M.Y.A.

W

hen next I fired the blunderbuss gun,
The recoil sent me to Permian time.
Dimetrodon was basking in the sun.
I saw him on the rocks after a climb,

His magnificent sail catching a ray.
That ol' chap was warming up for the hunt
With two rows of teeth sharply on display.
Silent in the morning, it made no grunt.

One thing I know from studying the facts,
The continents were all fused into one.
Pangea, 'tis called, this unified tract,
A million years it lasted 'till done.

The walkabout had me all tuckered out.
I needed a nap before my next bout.

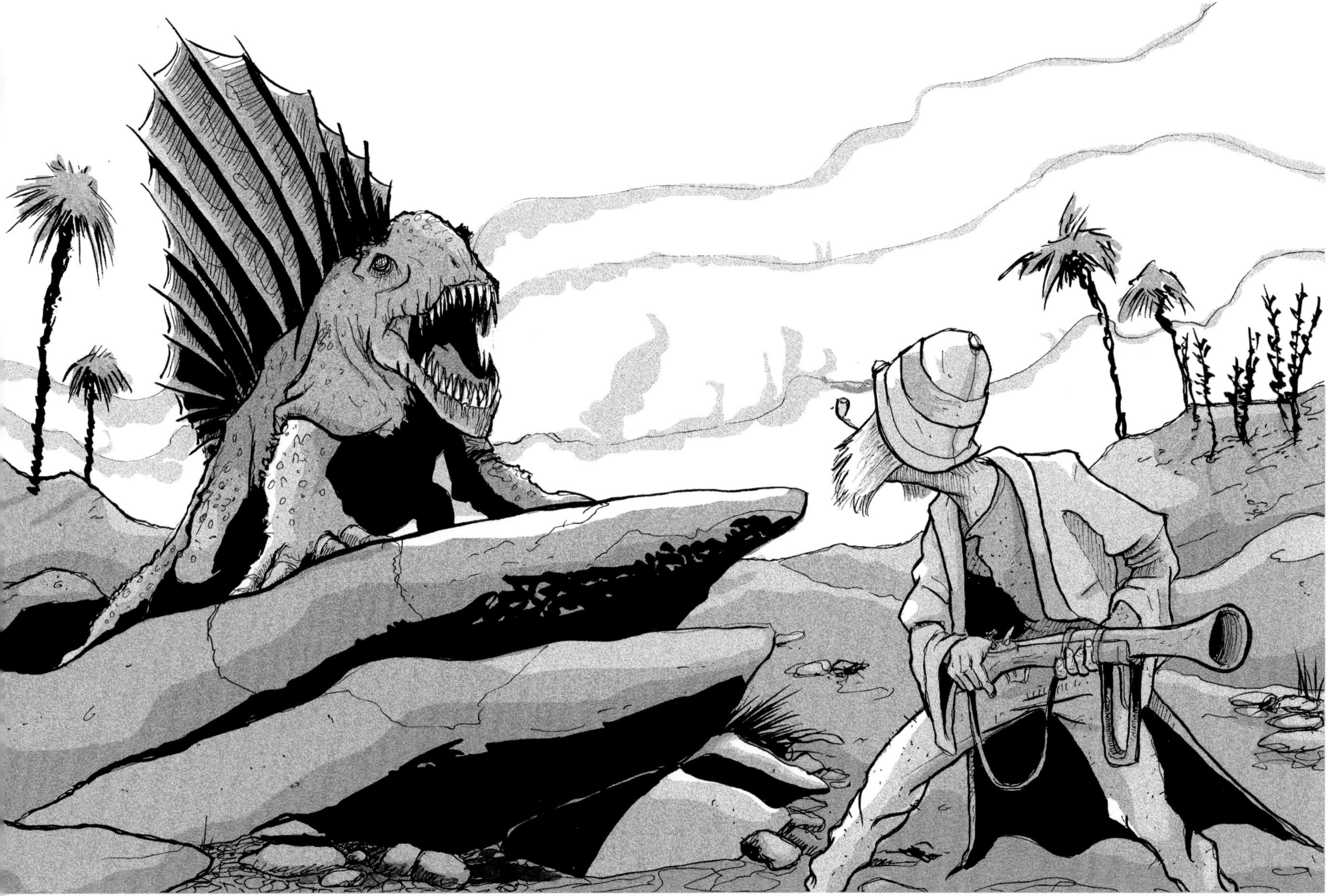

Permian
280 M.Y.A.

I awoke from this slumber much surprised.
Many things happened while I was asleep.
The "Great Dying" went on, I have surmised,
For reverence of life, a tear I did weep.

That which I saw with mine own eyes be true.
Combined with what I'd learned in a textbook.
This was a point when life hit a snafu.
I stayed around to give it a good look.

Death on the left and more death on the right.
Seven out of ten land families were gone.
What remained pushed on with all of its might.
Or we, ourselves, may not have come along.

No longer could I stay, it was too much.
A time with more life, I needed to touch.

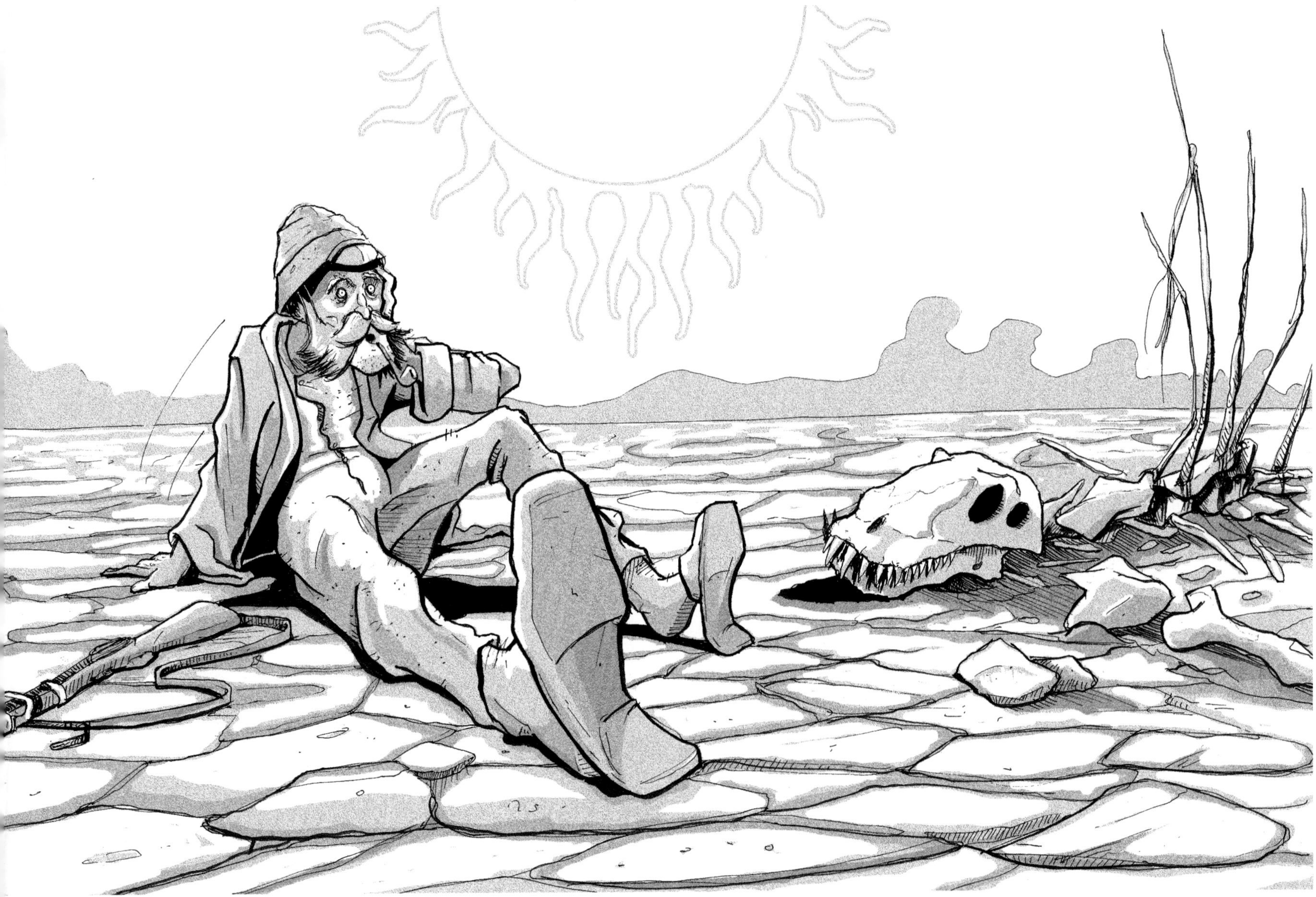

Permian
252 M.Y.A.

Next in the Triassic I got my wish.
I was besieged by fast little buggers,
No matter how hard I tried to vanquish.
They were too great in number to clobber.

The Mesozoic era had begun,
Although it took thirty million long years.
New life had arisen from extinction.
'Twas the beginning of Dinosaur peers!

The Dinos did not yet have the world stage.
The Synapsids, mammal-like reptiles,
Were stars in the early part of this age
Until they died out into Earth's files.

It was time to move on, that much I knew.
I pulled the trigger without much ado

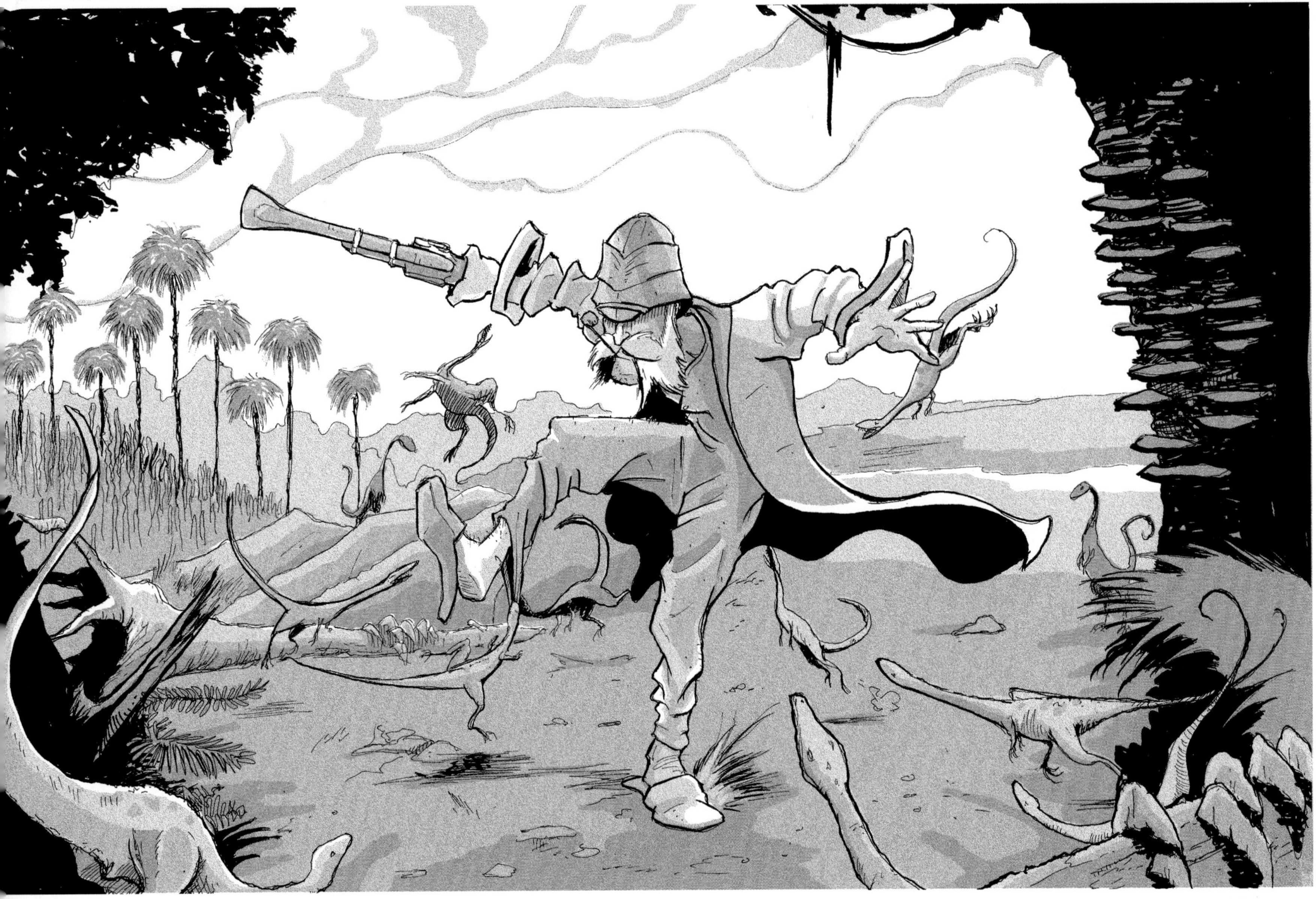

Triassic
225 M.Y.A.

I then found myself in the Jurassic;
High up in the nook of a redwood tree.
This view of mine was very fantastic.
You would not believe the sights I could see.

I was visited by a Sauropod—
It was a tall hungry Diplodocus.
On the green branch I extended, it gnawed.
Close to the beast, I was calm, not nervous.

Sliding from the trees to the ground below,
The first feathered friend I saw on this trip,
The Archaeopteryx, put on a show
For the lineage of bird's early kinship.

The weather was fine—I stayed there all day,
'Till I recoiled and went on my way.

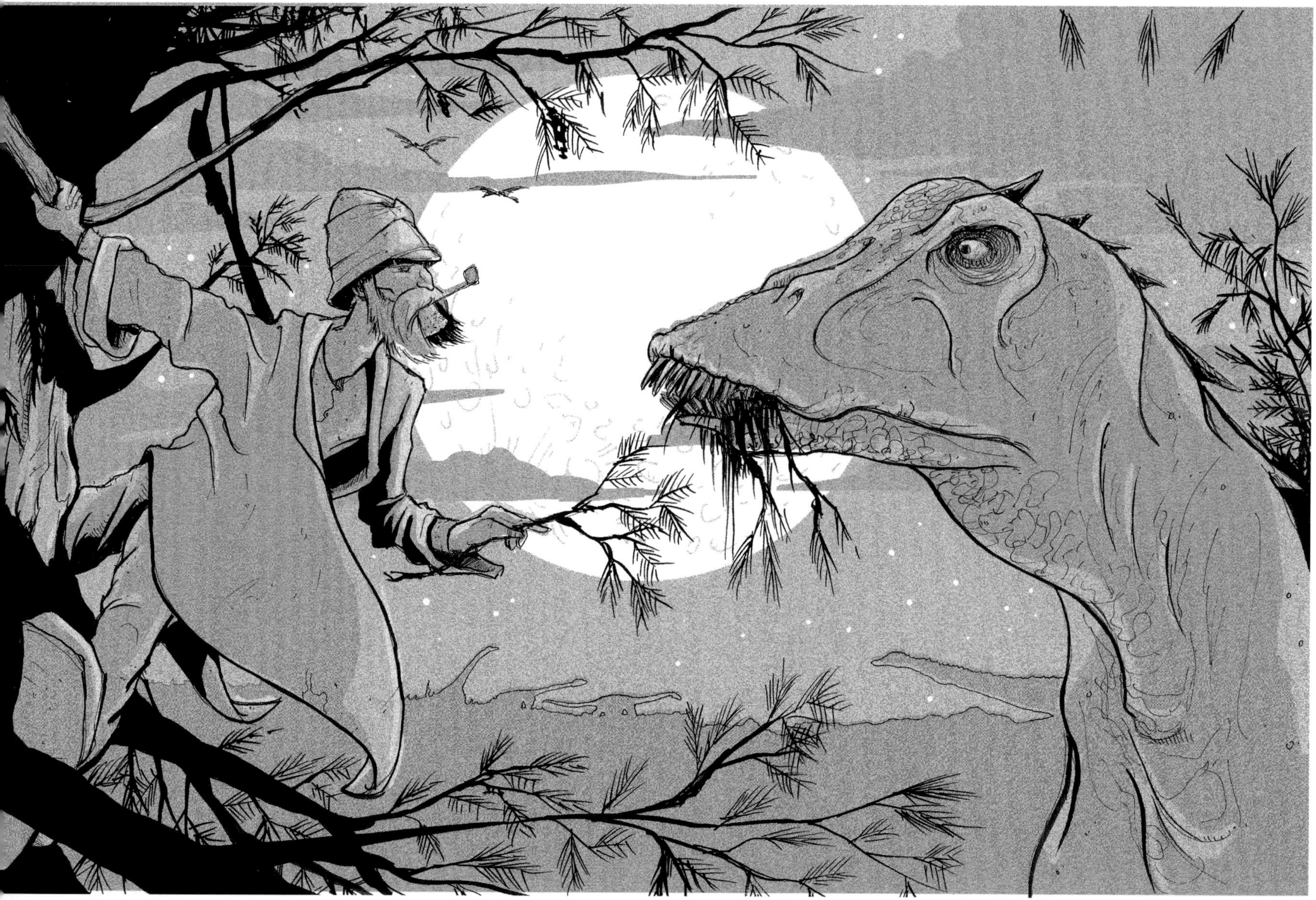

Jurassic
190 M.Y.A.

When I beheld the Cretaceous landscape
What first caught my eye were the flowering trees
Over which magnolia blooms did drape.
All about 'twas buzzing of early bees.

Note my wonderment was not long lasting.
Soon, through the bushes, a thundering sound
Alerted me I best be fast acting.
It was T. rex, like a snarling hellhound.

There was much more I would like to have seen,
But sightseeing is hard when on the run.
I didn't want to be Dino protein,
Whilst my heart was pounding like a piston.

I bid farewell to Tyrannosaurus.
If you want a rhyme, grab a thesaurus.

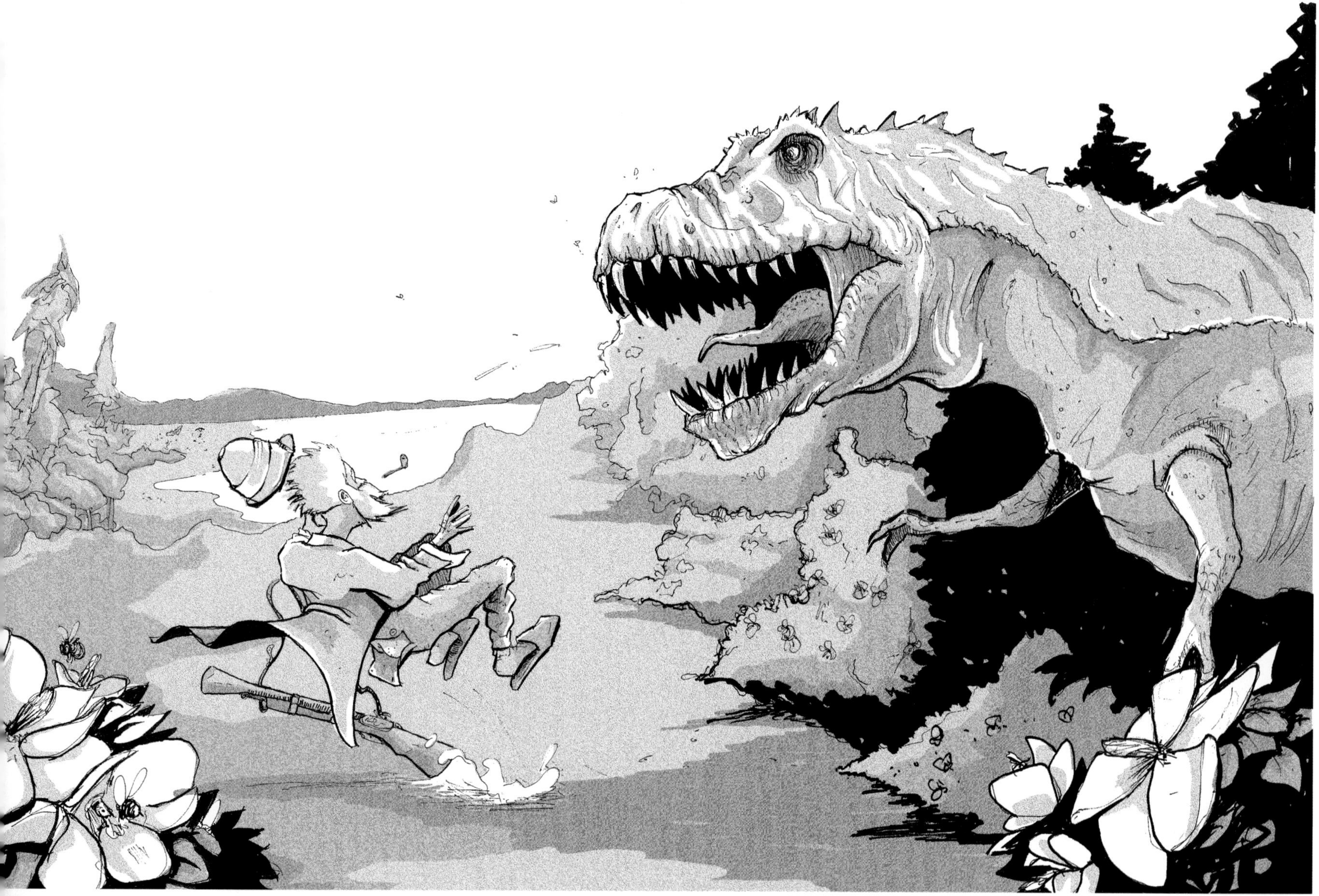

Cretaceous
135 M.Y.A.

My escape was but a few moments old,
My adrenaline still turned on eleven,
When I saw the greatest sight to behold—
A meteorite falling from heaven.

I knew this was the end of the dinos
For when that giant bolide makes impact,
Evolution's chorus hits a high note,
Then crashes down and begins a new track.

I did not stick around to see the crash.
The earth was to change, and change really quick.
I can proclaim with out being abash
I left the scene without further antic.

The Mesozoic had come to a close,
Drawing in my mind a vivid tableaux.

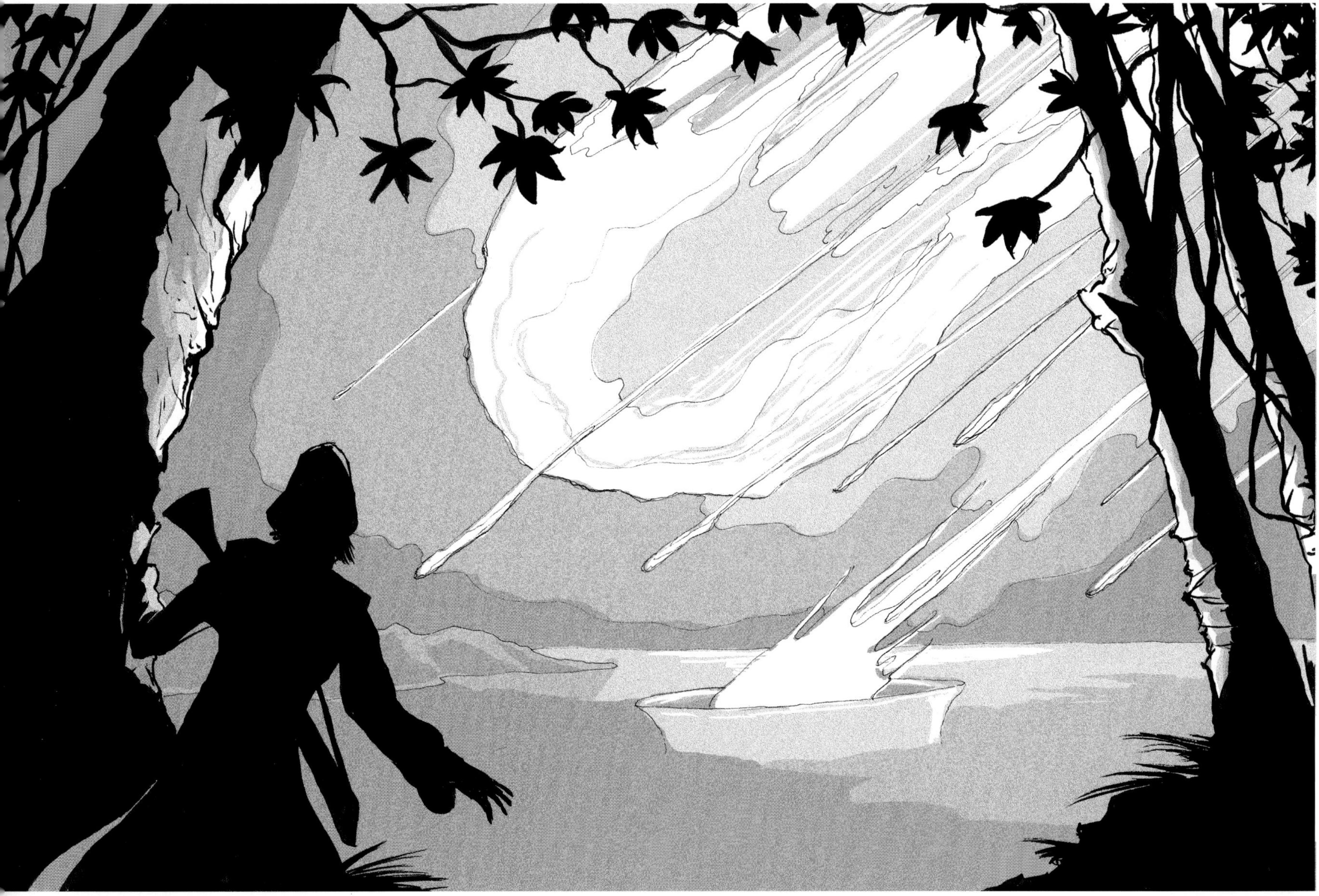

Cretaceous
65 M.Y.A.

Millions of years ahead in the Tertiary,
I found a world crowded with new mammals—
Some rather strange and others quite scary.
Each has a place in history's annals.

Oh, to give thought and remember them all,
But with a name like Gomphotherium
The feat of memory would not be small.
Learn Latin to avoid delirium.

I saw the early ancestors of man,
Australopithecus, the modern name.
One searched through my pocket with hairy hand.
I do admit to enjoying this game.

Ah, but once again I knew I must go.
I leveled the gun and shot with gusto.

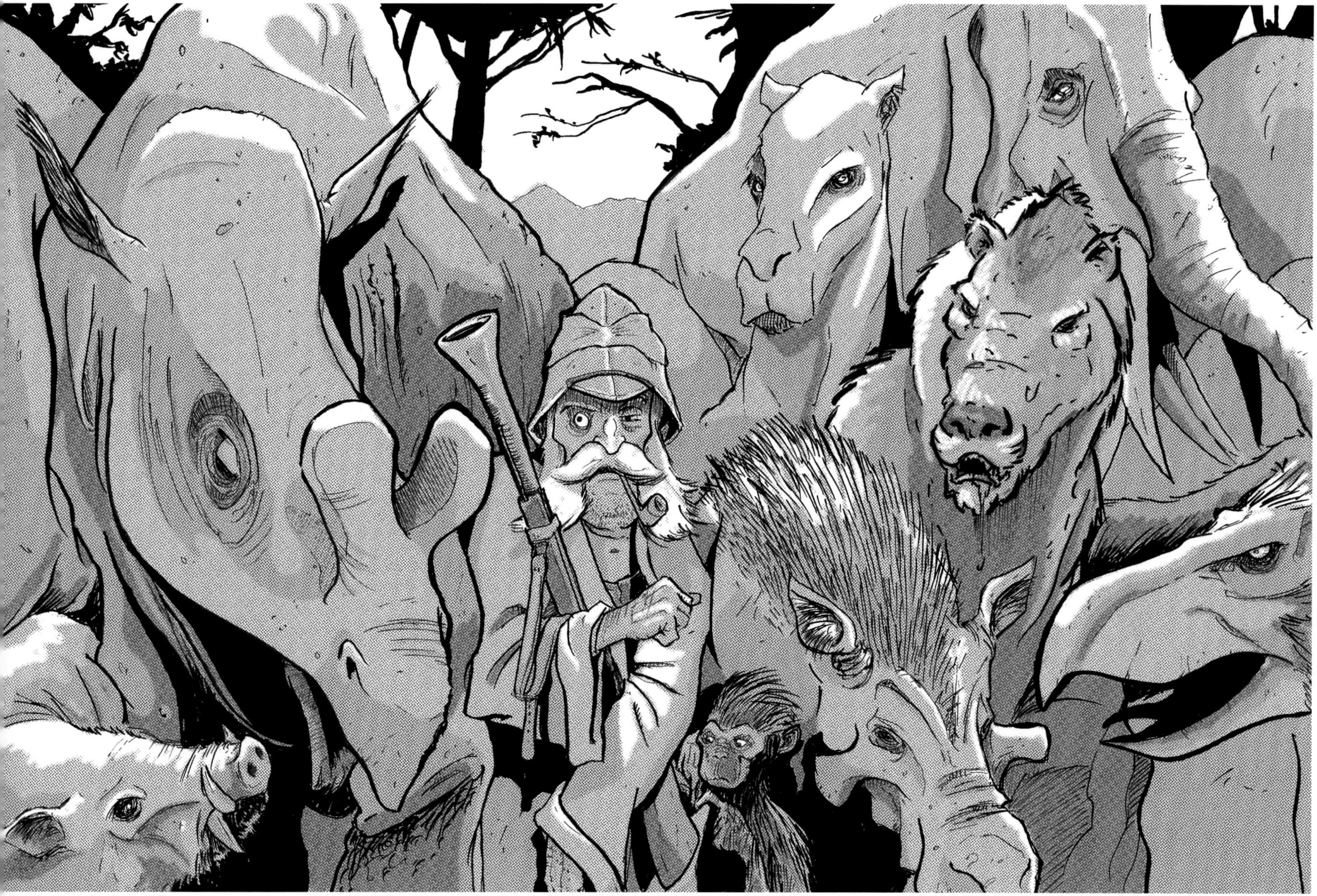

Paleogene
65 M.Y.A.

It was cold at my next destination,
My feet did shiver inside my slippers.
There must have been ice across the nation—
The Pleistocene was no place to nicker!

You had to be tough to live in this time
With no guns or bows to hunt the Mammoth.
Spear hunting with atlatl was in its prime,
Skill was key to bring down the behemoth.

Within the tribe they all worked together
To hunt or to gather the stuff of life,
No matter how horrible the weather.
The job would get done despite any strife.

I'm thankful these people did what they do,
For man's natural knowledge did accrue.

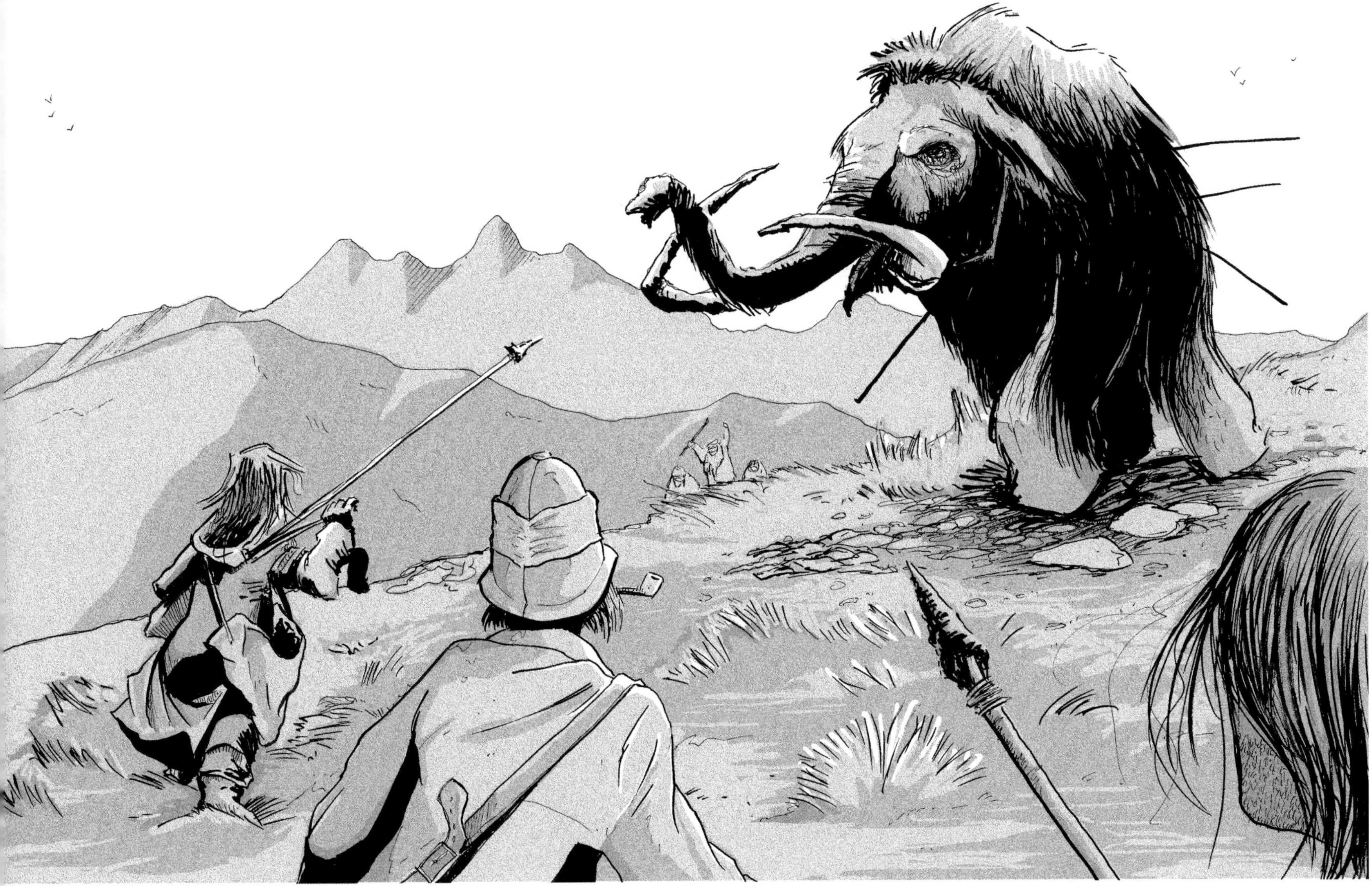

Pleistocene
2 M.Y.A

My next leg of this time travel journey
Took me to a land of pyramid mounds
Clustered within a green river valley
Dotted with fields where the maize did abound.

You may think I was in old Mexico,
But I could tell by the leaves of buckeye
I was close to the river Ohio.
This culture is known as Mississippi.

The people in the Holocene spread far,
From Michigan to Louisiana.
They anticipated the morning star,
And had cities larger than Viana.

But they disappeared before de Soto,
Leaving very much we do not know.

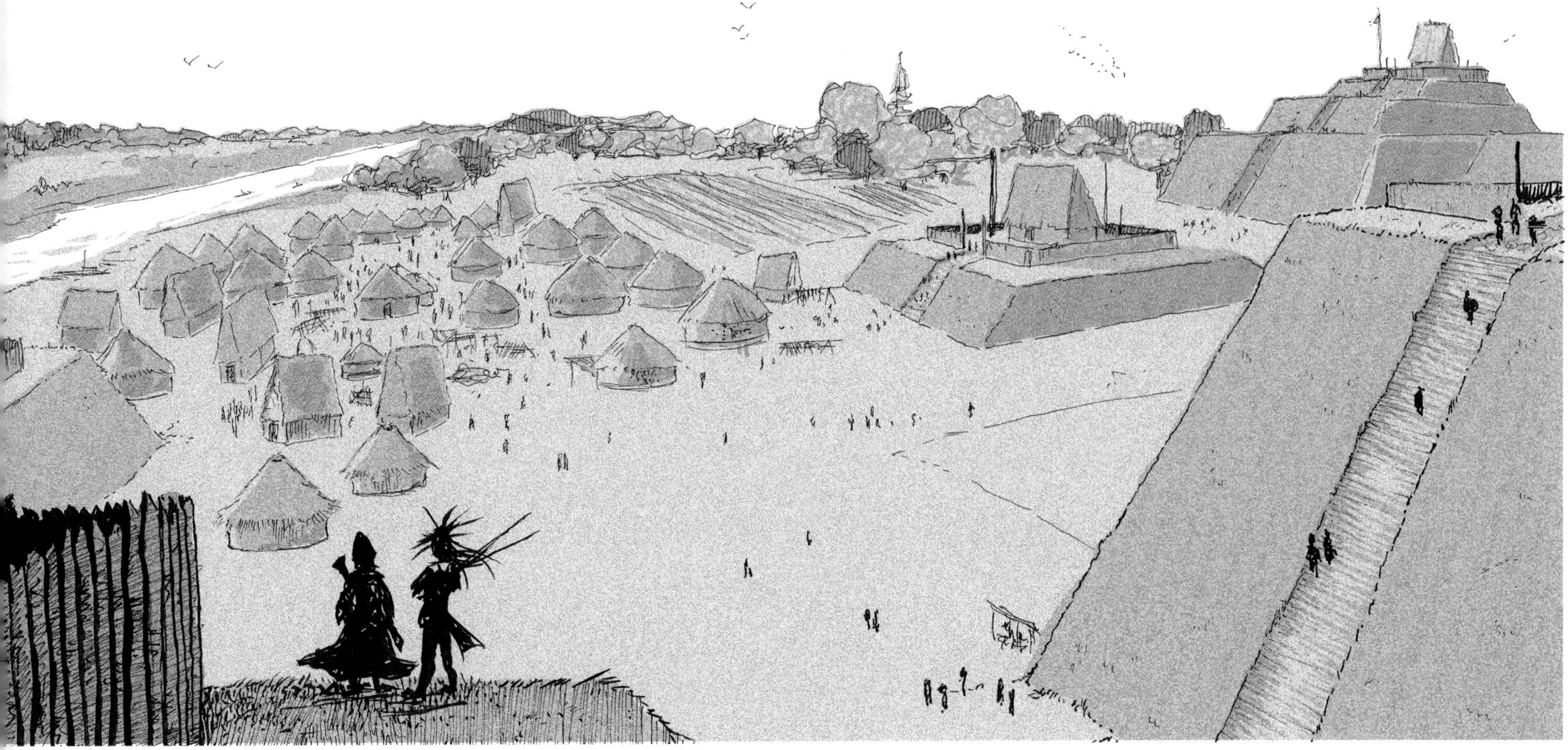

Holocene
1,215 Y.A.

With the last shot of my blunderbuss gun,
The recoil sent me to my native time,
Though it seemed as though I had just begun
If I were to measure by my clock chime.

I sat for a moment in amazement
And replayed the adventure in my head.
I knew the skeptics would call me flippant,
And contest with every word I said.

So I set it all down for the record,
This travelogue of time you have just read.
I do believe the facts are in accord.
Your Earth studies I wouldn't have mislead.

Now my story has been written and told—
I've a blunderbuss for those who be bold!

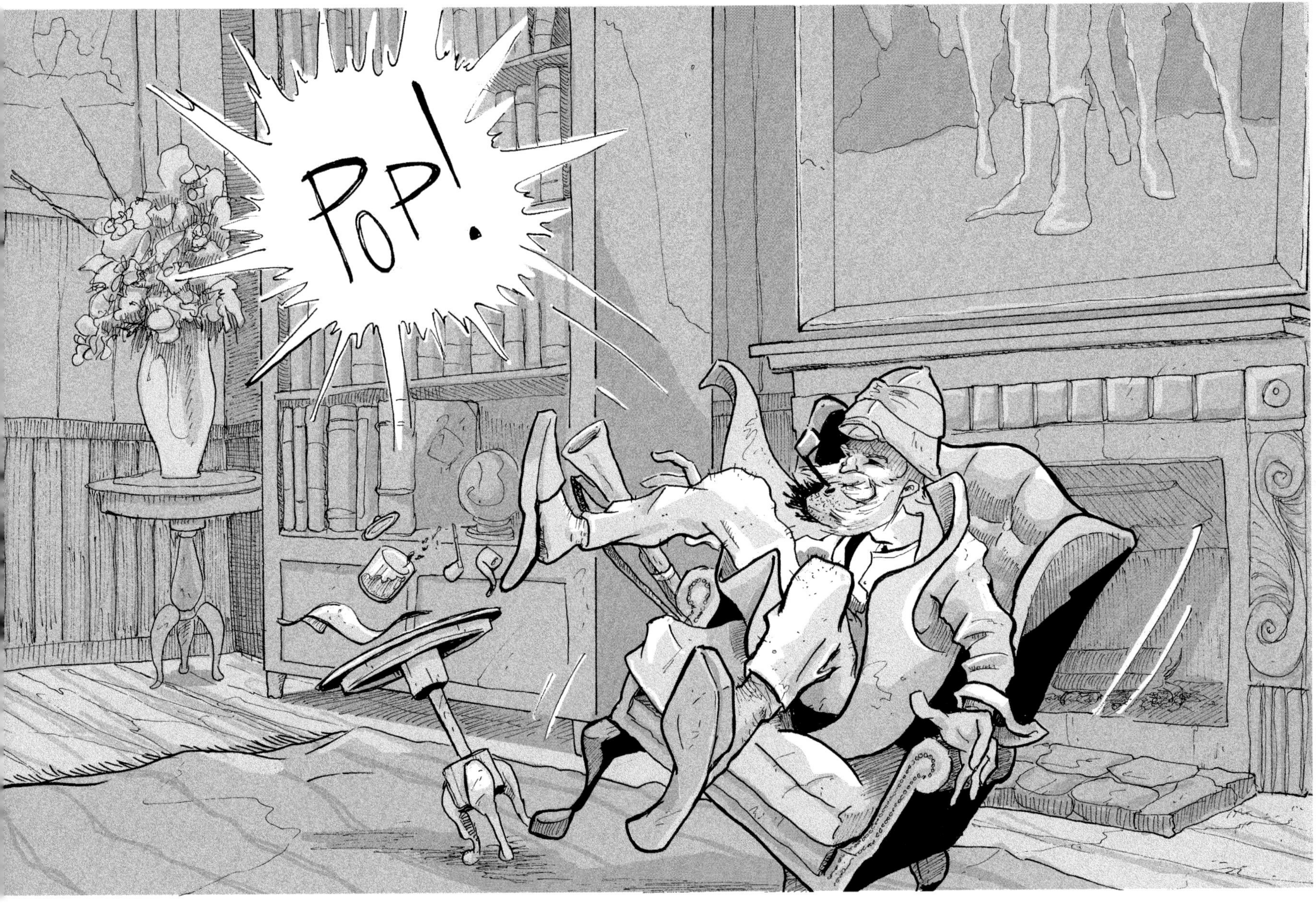
POP!

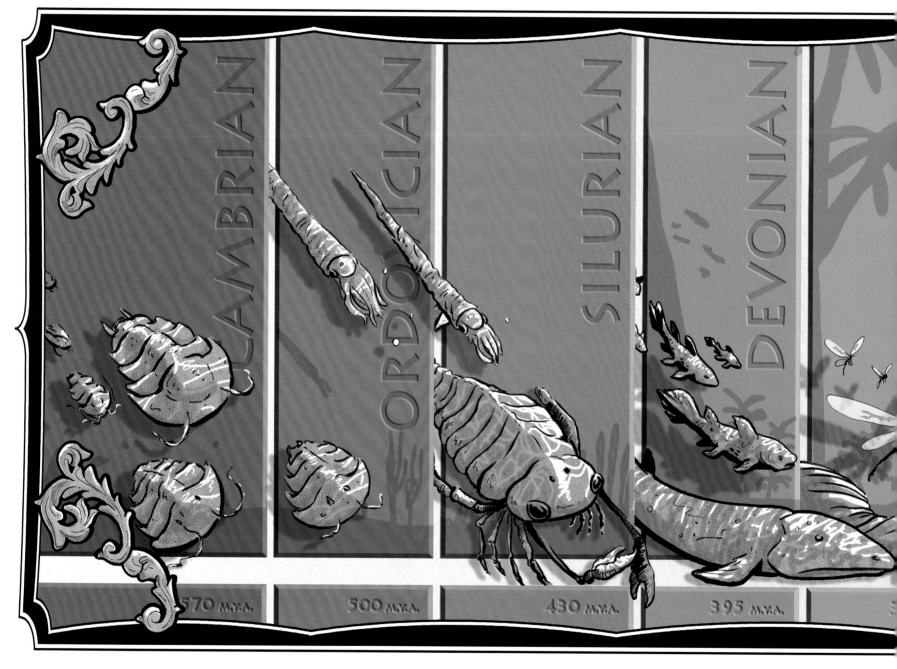

CAMBRIAN

ORDOVICIAN

SILURIAN

DEVONIAN

570 M.Y.A.

500 M.Y.A.

430 M.Y.A.

395 M.Y.A.

PERMIAN

TRIASSIC

JURASSIC

280 m.y.a.

225 m.y.a.

190 m.y.a.

PERMIAN

TRIASSIC

JURASSIC

225 m.y.a.

190 m.y.a.

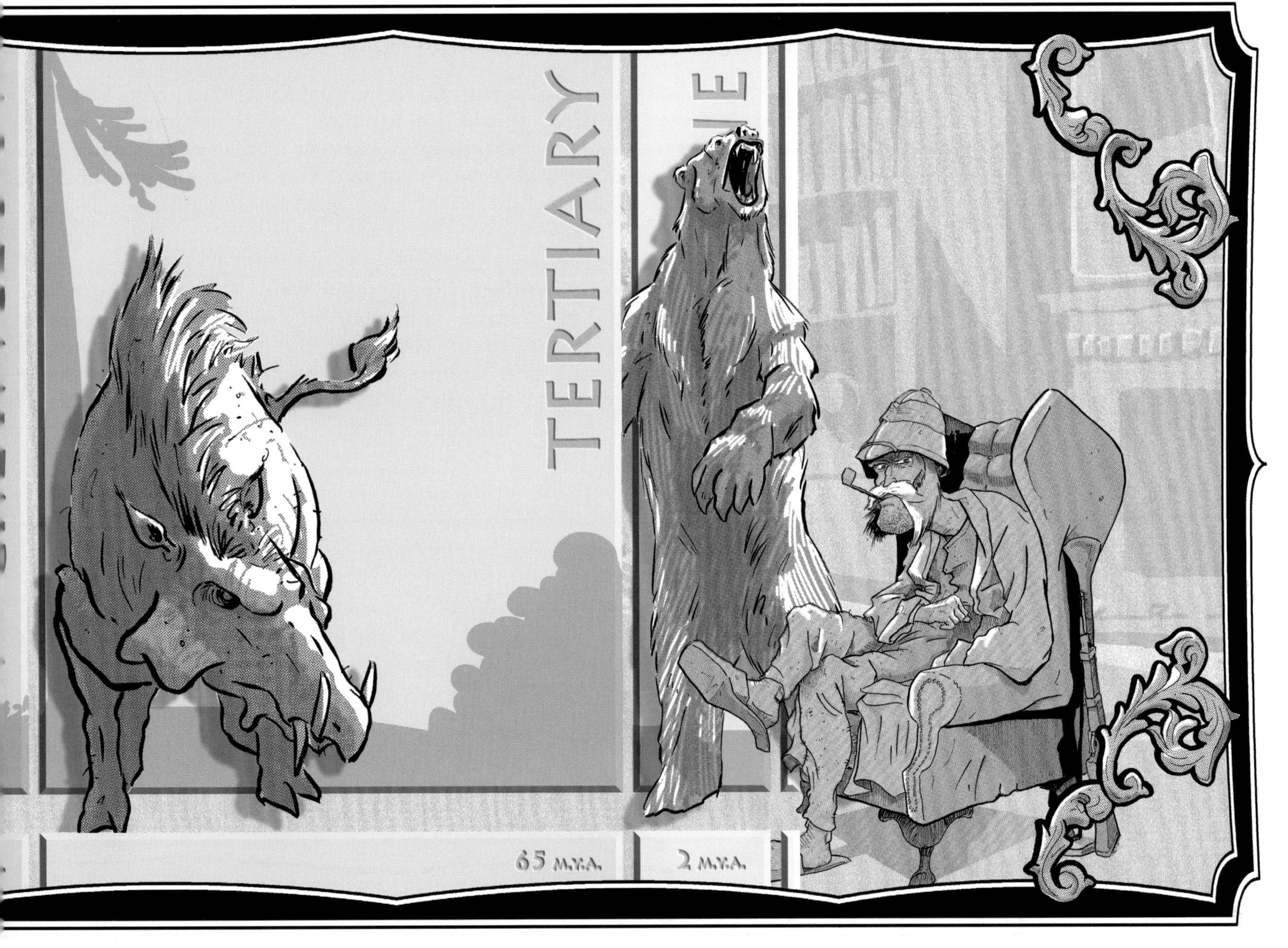
TERTIARY
65 M.Y.A.
2 M.Y.A.

Writer David R. Shapiro is the founder of Craigmore Creations. He has worked as an animal tracker, interpretive guide, youth educator, and summer camp director. David is the author of the Terra Tempo graphic novel series and several children's picture books. He lives in Portland, Oregon, and still working out the kinks in time travel.

Illustrator Christopher Herndon has been feeding himself by way of the funny book industry for over a decade. He is the creator of two comic book series and illustrator for numerous album covers, games, and magazines. He illustrated the Terra Tempo series, a children's book called *Tool. Time. Twist.*, and the comic, *Living with Zombies*. Herndon currently lives in Portland, Oregon. His mother still puts his drawings on her refrigerator.